Animals should definitely not wear clothing.

Written by Judi Barrett

illustrated by Ron Barrett

Atheneum Books for Young Readers
New York   London   Toronto   Sydney   Singapore

For Amy and Valerie

Atheneum Books for Young Readers
An imprint of Simon & Schuster Children's Publishing Division
1230 Avenue of the Americas, New York, New York 10020
Text copyright © 1970 by Judi Barrett
Illustrations copyright © 1970 by Ron Barrett
The text for this book is set in Futura.
Printed in Hong Kong
17 19 20 18 16
Library of Congress catalog card number: 70-115078
ISBN 0-689-20592-9

Animals should definitely not wear clothing...

because
it would be
disastrous for
a porcupine,

because
a camel
might wear it
in the wrong
places,

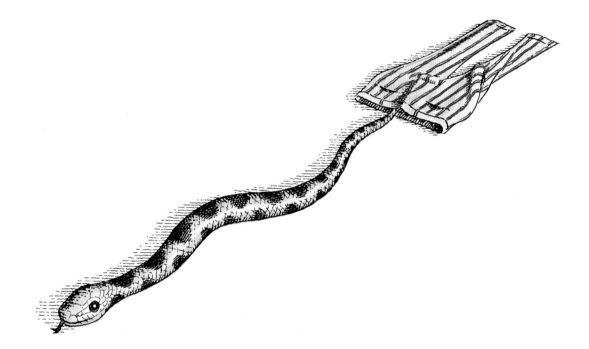

because
a snake would
lose it,

because
a mouse
could get lost
in it,

because
a sheep
might find it
terribly hot,

because
it could be
very messy
for a pig,

because
it might
make life hard
for a hen,

because
a kangaroo
would find it
quite

unnecessary,

because
a giraffe
might look
sort of silly,

because
a billy goat
would eat it
for lunch,

because
it would always
be wet
on a walrus,

because
a moose
could never
manage,

because
opossums
might wear it
upside down
by mistake,

and most of all, because it might be very embarrassing.

Judi Barrett divides her days between teaching art to children and writing children's books.

Ron Barrett spends his nights illustrating the books she writes, and his days as an Art Director at a New York advertising agency.

Animals should definitely <u>not</u> wear clothing is their second book. Their first one was *Old MacDonald Had An Apartment House.*

They both firmly believe that animals should definitely not wear clothing, except for an occasional dog coat on below freezing days.

This is where they draw the line.